RED TED
AND THE
LOST
THINGS

For Emile, Elsie
and Emma ~ M.R.

For the lost and found
of Dalston ~ J.S

First published 2009 by Walker Books Ltd,
87 Vauxhall Walk, London SE11 5HJ

10 9 8 7 6 5 4 3 2 1

Text © 2009 Michael Rosen. Illustrations © 2009 Joel Stewart

This book has been typeset in Opti Typo Roman and Regular Joe

Printed in China

British Library Cataloguing in Publication Data: a catalogue record for
this book is available from the British Library

ISBN 978-1-4063-1037-5

www.walker.co.uk

RED TED
AND THE
LOST
THINGS

MICHAEL ROSEN

JOEL STEWART

WALKER BOOKS
AND SUBSIDIARIES
LONDON · BOSTON · SYDNEY · AUCKLAND

One day a little bear called Red Ted was left on a train. He found himself being put on a shelf by a Man in a Hat...

Up you go!

4

Where am I?

You're in the Place for Lost Things.

But I was on a train with Stevie. We were going to her nan's. Then she got up and left me on the seat...

...and someone put you in a bag and here you are. It's always like that.

It'll be all right. Stevie will come and find me. She loves me as much as she loves cheese.

I thought I could smell cheese!

It's no use crying. She can't hear you.

So Red Ted, who was a brave little bear, stopped crying.

Next morning,
when the
Man in the Hat
came in,
Red Ted hopped
down off the shelf.

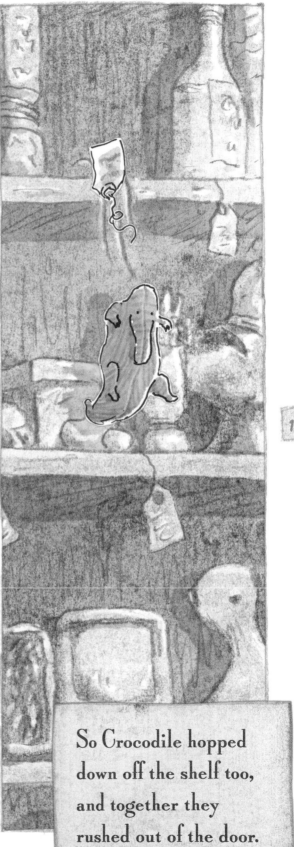

13

So Crocodile hopped down off the shelf too, and together they rushed out of the door.

And they followed the signs.

Over there!

WAY OUT

Outside, Red Ted stopped.
So Crocodile stopped.

We're still lost, aren't we? I knew things would go wrong.

It won't stay like this. Something will happen.

And just then a voice said:

It was a cat.

And the cat turned to go.

But then she stopped and sniffed.

Do I smell cheese? Mmmmmmmmm, lovely!

I think I know where your home is. Follow me.

So they followed the cat, and as they walked along she sang a little song:

I'm a cat
And I do
as I please,
I'm a cat
And I love
cheese!

After a while
it began to rain.

And they did.

When the rain stopped,
they walked on.
Under a bridge.
Through the market.
Down an alley.

So Crocodile showed
the great big dog his
great big teeth.

The great big dog didn't like Crocodile's
great big teeth and it ran away.

You were
very brave, dear boy,
very brave indeed!

Was I?

27

They walked on and came round a corner.

Red Ted stopped.

You're lost again, aren't you? You don't know where we are.

I do! I do!

All three of them rushed up to the front door.

But there was nobody home.

Things were looking bad.

Then, suddenly, round the corner, came ... Stevie!

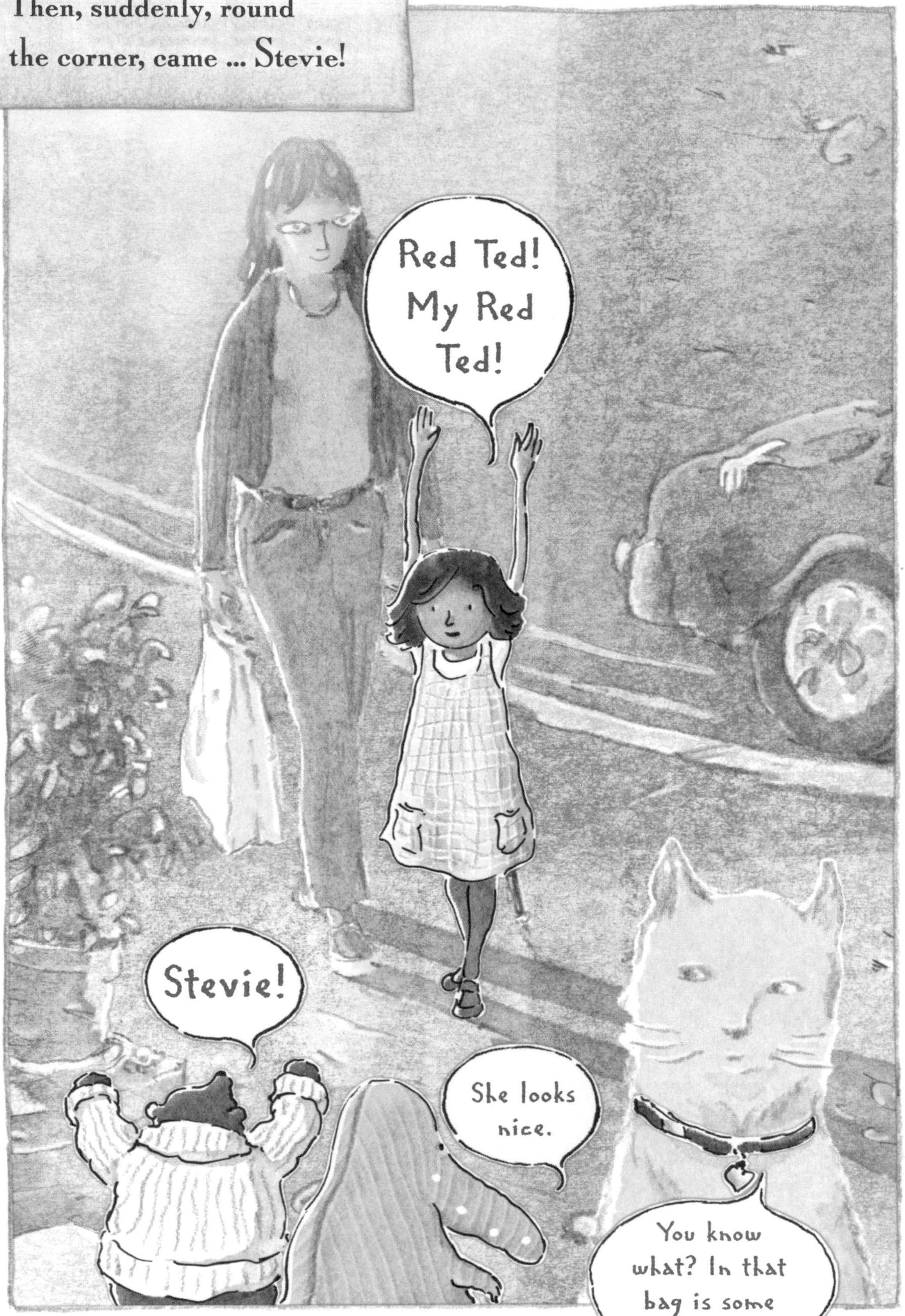

That night when she went
to bed, Stevie was happy.
Crocodile was happy.
The cat was happy.
But no one was happier
than Red Ted, who'd found
Stevie again and who wasn't
lost any more.